C000064346

Oh My Godalming

Ben Dobson

This book is licensed for your personal enjoyment only. This book may not be re-sold or given away to other people. If you would like to share this book with another person, please purchase an additional copy for each recipient. Thank you for respecting the hard work of this author.

Some names and identifying details have been changed to protect the privacy of individuals.

Copyright 2015 Ben Dobson
Cover: Louis Fryer & JP Croissant
Formatting: JP Croissant

Massive thanks to Godalming residents.
Without you there simply wouldn't be a book.

And of course, to you the reader. I
hope it raises a smile or two.

A Very Brief History

First and foremost, this is not a history book, there are plenty of other resources available that recount Godalming's past in a far more comprehensive manner. The reason for this background to be included is eloquently encapsulated by Carl Sagan's simple quote, 'You have to know the past to understand the present.' As limited as it is, it's hoped that the following goes some way in achieving that.

Godalming. God-al-ming. It seems a lot of people have enormous difficulty pronouncing the word. Maybe that's not so surprising given that the word is Saxon and translates as 'of the family or clan of Godhelm.' Residents then were known as Godhelmians whereas today the locals affectionately refer to themselves as 'mingers', which just happens to be an accurate reflection of many. Although the town was first recorded in the will of King Alfred the Great in 899, archaeological digs suggest the site was selected a couple of hundred years earlier, probably due to its well-drained land above the meadows of the River Wey.

The towns iconic Pepperpot, or Old Town Hall which has stood on the same site in one form or another for the past thousand years has, in its chequered history, been the local courthouse, the venue for important public announcements and home to 98 French prisoners of war. The current building is only a couple of hundred years old and is considerably smaller than its many predecessors as its purpose has been significantly reduced. On odd weekdays it hosts a fruit and vegetable stall, is the stage for the local GOLO draw and a shelter for adolescents waiting for buses home. With its gaudy pink paintwork, dingy lighting and lonely bench it's a popular place to eat, throw and throw up takeaways at the end of a night's revelling. Following mornings reflect the night before with discarded wrappers and remnants of kebabs plain to see. You can't polish a turd as the saying goes, but you can adorn it with hanging baskets it seems. Along with the occasional whiff of stale urine and scribbled graffiti it's sad, far-cry from what was once the most respected building in town.

From its very earliest roots Godalming has been a thriving town, continually reinventing its fortunes throughout the ages. In the Domesday book of 1086, 'Godalminge' is noted for its three successful water mills before branching out and becoming better known for the manufacturing of woollen cloth. Evidence of its woolly past can still be seen today in street names such as Woolsack Way and even in the town's coat of arms.

In the 17th century, the wool trade declined and so the progressive town switched to the knitting of stockings, still using wool but also silk and later, cotton. For generations, Godalming was synonymous for the quality of its knitwear and proof of this was when the body of George Mallory, the mountaineer and master at Charterhouse School, was recovered in 1999, he was wearing intact knitwear from W.F Paine, 72 Godalming High Street.

The town is well situated midway between London and Portsmouth and, as a result, had a booming trade from merchants and tradesman travelling along the route. Sailors, tailors, poachers and plumbers, tanners, planners, threshers and thatchers all made frequent journeys to and from the coast, often stopping over night in the town's plentiful inns. The Red Lion Inn and The Kings Arms, both on the High Street, did particularly well with the passing custom, regularly hosting up to 5000 horses nightly. According to the town's records, enough gunpowder was produced from their manure to defeat Napoleon, although it fails to mention the workings of this bizarre statistic. In 1698, The Kings Arms played host to Peter the Great and his entourage prompting the town's council to issue a warning to 'mingers' of the visitors' drunken, scandalous, late night activities. A plaque outside commemorates his stay but strangely omits the debauchery that ensued. Today, The Kings Arms has a colonial, safari feel to it with artificial hunting trophies hanging on the restaurant's bamboo wallpaper. It's reminiscent of a scene from 'Carry on up the Kyber' and at any minute Kenneth Williams will tip-toe through in his khaki uniform, whip under arm.

1881 was a tremendous year for Godalming. Not only did the Old Carthusians(Charterhouse old boys)win the F.A cup final 3-0, the town also became the first in the world to install public electricity for street lighting. Another plaque celebrates this feat. Unfortunately, it was to enjoy it for only three years as Siemens, who held the contract, deemed it financially unviable and reverted the town back to gas lighting. It would be another twenty years before Godalming once again had a public electricity supply.

The town also played an active role in the First World War. Aside from losing 105 souls to the

Hun, the good people of Godalming took in 35,720 articles of clothing from 8,930 soldiers camped on Witley Common, effectively turning the borough into a giant laundry. An extract from the Surrey Advertiser, dated 1915 reads,'During the past week, the gardens of many poorer people in the district have been filled with lines holding soldiers' underclothes.' One woman bravely took in the undergarments of a staggering 200 soldiers. It must have been quite a sight for the neighbours, underwear of all varieties zig-zagging around the garden, through the house and out through the front door. Maybe she had created the worlds first bio-hazard bunting? Considering the town's obsession with plaques, it seems unjust that this superhuman effort is not recognised with one. Nowadays, if Godalming was required to do the same, I suspect the powers that be would have something to say and would probably try to farm that responsibility out to the neighbouring parishes, thus keeping Godalming's aesthetics intact.

Despite their town being turned into a huge wartime washing machine, 'mingers' are on the whole a forgiving bunch and not ones to hold a grudge. Testament to this is the twin-town status Godalming shares with Mayen in Germany and Joignay in France. This three-way relationship is intended to promote an exchange of language, culture, friendship and tolerance, although this is still to be truly authenticated.

More recently, Godalming has grabbed headlines for a more...titillating reason. In 2012, 'Lovehoney', an online sex toy retailer conducted a survey and reported the town third for its online sex toy sales. Again, where's the plaque? Spending per head came in at 58p whereas Greater Manchester spent a measly 17p per head. With a population that currently stands at around 22,000 which includes children and OAP's, some residents must have impressive, if not intimidating, under the bed collections. The next time you're sitting next to a young mother in one of the coffee shops, don't necessarily assume that the buzzing is coming from a nearby mobile or the coffee machine.

Godalming's Greatest

Individuals are just as important as the history in shaping a town and if some past notable residents are anything to go by, it's clear to see how Godalming has become the proud town it is today.

It seems you can't go five yards without being reminded that Jack Phillips once frequented the area. Pubs are named in his honour as are memorials. Many buildings seem to have a connection to him in one way or another, all eagerly displaying plaques whenever they can. For those who don't know who Jack Phillips was, and there can't be many, he was the hero chief wireless telegraphist of the doomed Titanic, famed for selflessly sending mayday messages until succumbing to a watery grave. It is said that those who did survive the tragedy, did so only because of Mr Phillips' magnanimous nature.

Perhaps lesser known, is the other local connection to the Titanic and Jack Phillips and that's Lord William Pirrie who in 1844, bought Lea Park, now known as Witley Park. With its underwater conservatory/smoking room/ballroom, complete with aquarium windows and 9000 acres, Lord

Pirrie was a wealthy man. He had partly acquired his fortune by being a master boat builder and had the poisoned honour of finalising the details for Olympic-size ships' designs, which of course included the 'unsinkable' Titanic. He was a paid up passenger for the fated, maiden voyage but on the morning of the ships departure complained of feeling unwell and decided not to travel, thus probably saving his life. Conspiracy theorists, join an orderly queue.

One of the most infamous people to have resided in the town is the brilliant Mary Toft. In September 1726, Mary, a 25 year old married, illiterate servant and as sharp as a marble, made national, headline news for giving birth to a collection of mind-bending objects. These included legs of a cat, a hog's bladder and 18 dead rabbits. That's not a typo: rabbits. So extraordinary was her case that the non-English speaking George I who was occupying the throne at the time, despatched his head surgeon to investigate. After witnessing a stillborn rabbit birth he confirmed Mary's case to be true and valid, taking her to London for more investigation. When threatened with painful internal examination, Mary declared the whole affair to be a hoax, revealing a porter had been paid to source the rabbits which she then inserted into herself before delivering them. She was briefly regarded as a magician, although the rabbits which she pulled, did not come out of a hat. Consequently, she was jailed for being a 'notorious and vile cheat' whilst the embarrassed medical practitioners became the laughing stock of the country. Mary returned to Godalming no richer, or brighter than when she had left and carried on with her life in relative obscurity, occasionally being hired by wealthy individuals to entertain guests at dinner parties. It is, without question, one of the most bizarre hoaxes the country has ever seen and for a short time, put Godalming firmly on the map.

Around the same period, General James Edward Oglethorpe, member of Parliament, philanthropist, prison reformer, fine wig wearer and all round good egg resided in the opulent Westbrook Manor (later known as Meath House). In 1733 he, along with another 114 plucky people, sailed to the newly discovered America to found the state of Georgia. He worked tirelessly and selflessly in establishing a fair and fruitful society, integrating both the settlers and the indigenous Indians with whom he had built a mutually respectful relationship. To this day Oglethorpe Court exists in Godalming and in Georgia, schools, parks, streets, businesses and even towns carry his name, such is the esteem in which he is still held. As a result, Godalming now shares a separate, special twin town relationship with Augusta and Savannah in Georgia and in tribute 'Friends of Oglethorpe' continue to promote friendships between the towns. It does seem somewhat coincidental that two of the towns biggest personalities, albeit from different spectrums, shared the same time together. Whether General Oglethorpe hired Mary for her particular skill set remains unknown, but it is more than likely that they rubbed shoulders at some stage.

Charterhouse School and its past pupils are certainly worthy of note. Originally established in London in 1611 before being moved to its current site in 1872, Charterhouse has been a leading independent school ever since. It was one of the original seven English public schools as defined by the Public Schools Act of 1868, taking it's place among other prestigious educational institutes such as Eton, Harrow, Rugby, Shrewsbury, Westminster and Winchester and as it stands, lies in seventh place for the most expensive school in the UK. The previously mentioned mountaineer George Mallory and Leonard Huxley, father of acclaimed writer Aldous Huxley, were both masters at the eminent public school. Incidentally, Aldous's wife, Julia Arnold, was the founder of the local independent school for girls, Priors Field, which still boasts being one of the finest in the country.

Amongst many other accolades, Charterhouse has educated three Victoria Cross winners and has seen Robert Baden-Powell, founder of the Boy Scouts' movement, Peter Gabriel, Tony Banks, Chris Stewart and Mike Rutherford of Genesis, Ralph Vaughan Williams, composer, William Makepeace Thackeray and both Dimbleby brothers to name but a few, passed through its hallowed doors. Interestingly, after a 2007 visit, Roy Hattersley, the former deputy leader of the Labour Party commented, '... Charterhouse educates men who are destined to rule the universe..' and concluded with '...it's existence allows the rich and powerful to ignore the world beyond its boundaries'. Jeremy Hunt also attended Charterhouse.

It seems that Godalming is blessed with outstanding schools and, in them, some astounding students. A tale told by one house master speaks volumes about the calibre of those that attend. It was a Tuesday afternoon and an alarm had been raised for a missing overseas pupil. Despite the school's best efforts, he was nowhere to be found and therefore assumed that he was no longer on school grounds. A couple of hours after the police had been informed the missing boy nonchalantly wandered back in, clutching a Harrod's bag and wondering what all the fuss was about. When questioned, he very matter of factly told them that he fancied a bottle of wine to go with his evening meal so had gaily jumped on a train to London. As his parents had always shopped at Harrods he was blissfully unaware that wine was available at other retail outlets. He reluctantly surrendered the wine and promptly made a phone call to his parents to share this latest revelation. By all accounts, it was quite a day for him.

In recent years, Godalming has been labelled 'Celebrity Central', due to the range of famous faces that were seen about town. Penelope Keith, Chris Evans, Anthea Turner, Ringo Starr, Brian May and Eric Clapton have all lived and shopped locally. Attracted by its visual appeal, Godalming has come to the attention of Hollywood producers. For example, 'The Holiday' was partly filmed in the town and nearby Bourne Wood has been the location for a number of blockbuster films such as Casino Royale, Harry Potter and the Half-blood Prince, Robin Hood, Gladiator and fairly recently, Warhorse. The town's even made it into comedy sketches. One of Cardinal Burns sloaney characters smugly introduces herself with 'Hi my names Rachel and I grew up in Godalming in Surrey', hitting the hoity-toity nail on the head.

Second only to the town's love affair with Jack Phillips is its admiration for the world renowned horticulturist Gertrude Jekyll. Widely regarded as 'the premier influence in garden design' both here in England and across the pond in the States, Jekyll's legacy throughout the town still attracts enthusiastic garden designers from all over the globe. During her illustrious career, she designed over 400 gardens including the eye catching Hestercombe gardens in Somerset, and closer to home, the glorious Jack Phillips Memorial Cloisters and the Rose garden at Prior's Field school. She enjoyed a particularly productive, professional relationship with the young, up and coming architect Edwin Lutyens and upon her request, Lutyens designed her house, Munster Wood, now known as Munstead Wood in Busbridge in 1896. It is still viewed as one of his early masterpieces. Gertrude died in 1932 and her tombstone in Busbridge Churchyard was fittingly designed by her friend Lutyens. In reference to her name, her brother Reverend Walter Jekyll was a good companion to none other than Robert Louis Stevenson, who used their family name in his timeless classic Dr Jekyll and Mr Hyde.

Julius Caesar, the cricketer not the Emperor was born here, as was Sam Worthington of Avatar fame, Ashley Cole once had a kebab from Godalming kebab House and probably left his mark one way or another in the Pepperpot and if rumours are to be believed, Russell Crowe saw Godalming from a passing train window.

Having had such reputed persons gracing Godalming's streets, it's safe to say that the town has been built on some solid, noble and rather unusual foundations. But Godalming doesn't need to bask in former glories, it's got it's modern day celebrities that are sure to make just as big an impact as any of the town's predecessors.

Highstreet Highlights

And so to today. Black bollards line the one way high street, preventing anything wider than the occasional bus or frequent Range Rover to pass down it. Timber framed buildings interspersed with faded, lettered brickwork nostalgically hint at a by-gone era. With over 230 listed buildings of all shapes and sizes almost every step has historical interest.

In 2007, the Guardian newspaper featured Godalming in its weekend supplement 'Let's move to...' and asked residents for their thoughts on the town. Milly Watts' quote is typical of the responses that came in:

'This must have been one of the few towns in the country where a massive supermarket can coexist with a vibrant independent shopping scene: admittedly the supermarket is no Tescos...it's a glorious Waitrose, and one of the largest in the country. This place is blessed.'

The article concluded with the case against – 'Oh, nothing really, except the unbearable smugness of life in the fat, comfy stockbroker belt and the extremely high cost of living and property. That's all. Terrible traffic, too.'

Despite the escalating rental prices, a few independent businesses still manage to survive such as the butchers and bakers. Sandwiched between the rare independents and the abundant charity shops, are the usual high street big boys, WHSmiths, Waterstones, Boots and of course, Wetherspoons. It's a mystery how Wetherspoons was able to slip under Godalming's town council radar when they are so vehemently opposed to any fast food outlet, discount stores or any other industry that might bring the town's good name into disrepute. Naming it in homage after Jack Philips probably had something to do with it. No doubt they're kicking themselves now when they see patrons of Wetherspoons staggering around at ten past eight in the morning, limp rollie dangling from their lips, arms waving, swearing at fictitious foes.

It was here, one lunchtime, that I was witness to an extraordinary scene that's indicative of high street spectacles. Shortly after taking a seat by the window, a large white van stopped abruptly, hazard lights blinking. The driver jumped out and hurried around to the back doors, traffic already building up behind him. He was joined by the butchers skinny apprentice who took the lead in opening the double doors. As soon as he had released the catch, the doors flew open and out fell a fully grown frozen pig, pinning the apprentice on the road under its stiff trotters. A gathering crowd looked on in disbelief as the apprentice squirmed in pain, trying to free himself from the hog on top of him. The van driver was a diminutive man, probably half the size of the beast and although the animal rocked, his shoulder barging made little impact. He then mounted the pig, arms around its neck and attempted a weird ju-jitsu move to try and topple the animal. This peculiar scene had by now attracted a sizeable audience. An audience that was happier to watch than to help. The Discovery driver directly behind the van, who had witnessed everything unfold, began honking. This only panicked the van driver who by now had positioned himself like a Mongolian horseman, leaning to the side, arms wrapped around the neck and knees squeezing the dead mammal's ample belly in an attempt to pull it off its hooves. Regardless of his best efforts, it was not to be moved. As the apprentice groaned under the pig, his fellow butchers joined the van driver and to a round of applause from the gathered masses finally managed to remove the pig and hurry it in to the shop leaving the apprentice flat out on the tarmac. The Discovery driver had had enough and rather than offering help to the stricken young man, manoeuvred his vehicle around him shouting expletives as he went. When a blanket and a pillow arrived, it was clear that the poor chap was in trouble and not going anywhere soon. Ten minutes ticked by before a siren was heard approaching but due to the combination of the traffic and swelling numbers of mustard corded spectators, it took the ambulance a further ten minutes to reach the scene. The closer the ambulance came the more reluctant the Barbour wearing bystanders were to move, determined not to lose their view, forcing the ambulance to negotiate the black bollards, the people and the casualty. The bollards and the people were safely avoided, but unfortunately for the young man, his outstretched right foot was a challenge too far for the ambulance driver. Onlookers covered their mouths as the casualty squealed again. The muttering locals only started to disperse once the semi-conscious youth had been put in traction and slid into the back of the ambulance, right leg heavily cast. It was just another day on Godalming's high street.

Events like these, are of course, only made possible by the people involved in them, so it's no wonder then such scenes are common with some of Godalmings wackiest characters wandering around. For instance, there's mad Maureen, an elderly resident who is known about town for her unique taste in footwear and her poor, ageing dog. She's been seen wearing a fisherman's wader on one leg and an open toed sandal on the other all the while leading a rather sorry looking terrier behind her. It's as if she's saving the terrier the trouble of pulling its own wormed bottom across the floor. It visibly winces when being pulled over the street's cobbles.

As time has passed Maureen's footwear has become more and more interesting. A swimming flipper and high heel, a trainer and a clog and most recently a thigh-high boot and a moccasin slipper which gave her the most curious walk, all with her faithful hound in tow. This time it wasn't the footwear that drew people's attention, it was her dog. As she hobbled around the shops, her dog seemed to bounce off corners and ricochet off walls. On closer inspection, the front legs simply weren't working. One passing, inquisitive dog, took a fateful sniff before beating a whimpering retreat, tail between its legs. Seemingly oblivious, mad Maureen continued to lurch from one foot to the other with such determination she failed to notice the stunned faces and gasps from passers-by. It's a shame that mad Maureen never knew Mary Toft; they would have got along famously. If it was possible to host a past and present Godalming dinner party, those two would definitely top the list.

Along with mad Maureen, there's a Joan Collins lookalike that bumbles around town. With her over-sized rimmed hat, Jackie Onassis sunglasses, cigarette holder and spray on gold leggings she dithers in the shops in such a way she always appears lost. She pushes to the front of queues, poking peoples eyes with her threatening hat, asking random, irrelevant questions before exiting and repeating the same in the next shop. If she's not on foot, she's in her convertible car, causing chaos by driving wherever she likes, including the wrong way down many of the town's one-way streets. If she is questioned or confronted on her behaviour, her first response is to go to her hand-bag and produce her Coutt's bankcard in an effort to buy her way out of trouble.

Another familiar sight on the high street is the friendly Big Issue seller. She stations herself in an alley-way next to Waterstones and politely greets each passer-by, hoping to off-load a copy of the latest edition. Godalming doesn't have too many immigrants, so it's interesting to watch the reaction of locals when they're offered something in a foreign accent. Youths drift by and apologetically decline, usually on the grounds of lacking money. The mothers pushing prams blank her, unimpressed that she is allowed to be there at all. The retired generation are the most amusing with many of the interactions being much the same.

Big Issue Seller: *(in fluent English)*: "Good morning Madam, good morning sir, Big Issue?"

(an elderly couple stop and smile politely)

Elderly woman: *(speaking slowly and loudly)*: "Good morning, and how are you today?"

Big Issue Seller: 'Very well, thank you Madam, it's a beautiful day. Big Issue?'

Elderly woman: "Do you like the weather in our country?"

Big Issue Seller: "Yes, it's very similar to the weather in my country. Big Issue?"

Elderly woman: "Oh I see. What is your country? This is England."

Big Issue Seller: "Romania. I have been in this country for five years. Big Issue?"

Elderly woman: "Did you come by boat? It's shocking what's going on over there. Quick Harold, give the poor dear some change."

Harold: *(whispering to his wife)*: "I haven't got any change. I've got a five pound note?"

She apologises and they both hurry off, busily discussing the conversation between themselves. For the seller, it's nothing new. It will be one of the dozen similar conversations she'll have to endure that day, and the next and the next after that. She's almost treated like a novelty act, there to entertain and remind residents there is a world outside Godalming.

There's one, wheelchair-bound, elderly gentlemen who is often seen in Godalming and around the surrounding area. He's an amputee but that hasn't stopped him having a remarkable life if you're to believe his heroics. These range from being the first man to swim the Atlantic unaided to being the inventor of the rolling pin. It was during my first conversation with him that my suspicions of his distinguished past were raised. In the space of three minutes, I had been called at least four different names, none of them being remotely accurate. Numerous meetings later, I'm still everyone but Ben, regardless of my constant corrections. A typical conversation with him would go something like this:

Him: "Hello Mark, you're looking well today."

Me: *"Ben.* Thank you, you're not
looking too bad yourself."

Him: "Well you know Tim, soldiering on. Did
I ever tell you when I was a soldier serving
her majesty, God bless her, in India?"

Me: "It's **Ben**. Yes, I think you have."

Him: "It's not like it is now John. We had
to get around on elephants back in them
days. You ever been on an elephant Tom?"

Me: *"It's*...yes I have."

Him: "Well Dave. It's like being on boat,
going from side to side. The natives said
I had an infinity with the animals."

Me: "Do you mean affinity?"

Him: "Yeah, that's right Ian, an infinity.
You know, I could talk to them."

He's Godalmings answer to Uncle Albert with
conversations lasting as long as you let them.
Polite strangers have been trapped for hours.

Apart from bemusing people with his fanciful
tales, such as the time he single handedly fought
off two hundred Germans in the First World War
with his bare hands, he relies on the good nature
of locals to assist him in most everyday activities.

On one such occasion he requested the help of a friend of mine and being a good man, agreed without hesitation. Fifteen minutes after asking, my friend returned ashen faced having spent the entire time in the toilet aiding the elderly gent in all aspects of bodily evacuations. Just when he had taken his seat, happy but scarred with his noble deed, he was called upon again, this time to give him a helping hand out of the pub. An hour later, he returned. When questioned about his whereabouts, he told us that after rolling him out of the pub he had requested further assistance to get him to the bus-stop. Once at the bus stop and thinking his duty was done, was then asked to help him onto the bus. Little did he know that the bus wasn't scheduled for another forty-five minutes and so he sat with him, politely listening to his escapades of when he served as an Air Force test pilot.

Considering he requires help in nearly everything he does, the distances he covers and where he ends up are staggering. He's been seen in local car parks with a pay and display ticket on the front of his wheelchair, Winkworth Arboretum and the strangest of all, parked on the A3's hard shoulder just outside Guildford. How he gets to these places is a mystery but I'm sure that if you asked him, his story wouldn't disappoint and would most likely involve either a parachute or aliens or maybe even parachuting aliens.

Coffee, Clubs and Pubs

With Godalming being a satellite town, a large number of its inhabitants make the daily commute to London. As expected, many share the same train to and from the capital and so small clubs have formed. One of the oldest clubs is the 18.18 club which departs Waterloo at, well, 18.18. Anyone can be a member of this prestigious club and they enthusiastically welcome new applicants. The only qualifying condition is that members agree to drink a shot of whiskey at every station that begins with a W. Looking at the train route, it doesn't seem that daunting, Waterloo, Wimbledon, West Byfleet, Woking, Worplesdon. Five shots in forty-five-ish minutes. In actual fact, the truth is only realised when you're on board and that every station begins with a W. Clapham junction becomes Wapham junction, Guildford Wuildford, Farncombe Warncombe and Godalming, appropriately enough becomes Wodalming. Eight shots in 45ish minutes; not so easy. The vast majority of first timers also are last timers with many having to be scooped out of the train by disgruntled partners. For the long-term members, this state has been catered for. Taxi drivers are pre-booked and generously tipped for 'assisting' their clients from the train to the taxi to then finally their front door. The 18.18 from Waterloo has been said to be similar to special forces selection; you can train and train but can never be prepared for how tough it will be. Those lucky few that do make it through wear their badge with pride, and if the stories are to be believed, it is only a few.

Whilst the commuters are slowly getting cirrhosis of the liver, their partners and young children shuffle around the town's many coffee shops. These young families gravitate towards each other and end up pushing princely prams from one coffee shop to the next, three abreast on the pavement, heedless to anything and anyone. A human battering ram if you will, squeezing people into the fringes. The children would have traces of the organic, free-range, gluten free, non-sugar, non-dairy blueberry muffin and fat-free 'babychino' down their tweed jackets and on the air bag that dominates the pram's hydraulic handlebar. I once had the pleasure of being behind a leather booted and wax hatted mother in her early forties. She was leaning at an almost impossible 45 degree on a coffee shop counter, legs and arms crossed, refusing to give way to coming and going traffic whilst in no uncertain terms telling the young, bewildered staff member about the moral obligation of the company to pay its taxes and demanded to know what he intended to do about it. Meanwhile, Henry and Henrietta (no word of a lie) were running amock pinching marshmallows off people's plates and slapping a pram bound toddler around the face. Having been reprimanded by the relevant parents, Henrietta screamed down the place drawing the immediate attention of the mother who then began to tell the parents that they should be ashamed of their behaviour and she had a good mind to report them to social services. At that she turned with Henrietta in hand and stomped out telling the staff member that he should expect an official complaint from her. Henry catches up only after he's pushed over two chairs and thrown a mobile across the room. They all bundle, coffee-less into the waiting Range Rover, ignoring the fruity language coming from the fuming motorists they had blocked in for the last fifteen minutes.

With so many of these young mothers roaming free, coffee shops are springing up all the time. As one closes, another opens. There's even one that doubles up as a Yoga studio. With such a range, the quality differs significantly. There's one coffee shop that proudly advertises its soup of the day as the best value in town. When enquiring which soup it was, the waitress cheerfully and rather confusingly replied 'The soup of the day can be whatever the customer wants it to be.' Her answer was only fully understood after she turned, opened the cupboard and proudly pointed to a row of tins, all labelled Heinz.

Ambitious coffee shop managers aren't the only people of whom you have to be vigilant. It's been known that some of the traders at the periodically held farmers markets have also been guilty of hefty price inflations. On occasion, rogue traders have been sighted in Waitrose filling baskets with produce that reappears on a stall a couple of hours later, albeit with a slightly different sticker and very different price tag.

Aside from the multitude of coffee shops and cafes, Godalming has its fair share of restaurants as well. Leading the pack is the Italian restaurant, La Luna, which is seen by many to be Godalming's and indeed Surrey's finest eaterie and with its exceptional reviews on both Trip Advisor and in The Good Food Guide, they may well have a point. In 2010, the Telegraph food critic, Matthew Norman, visited La Luna but thought otherwise, scoring it a lowly 3/10. His ensuing article caused such outrage from 'mingers' that a couple of months later, the Telegraph ran a section exclusively on just the comments. There were calls for Mr Norman's immediate dismissal as well as threats to boycott the newspaper entirely despite the customers' 50 year loyalty to it. A cautionary tale to other restaurant reviewers then, degrade La Luna and the locals will be baying for your head on a beautifully whittled stick.

Opposite the stuffed Waitrose car park, stands a 17th century congressional church, occupied now by the Bel and The Dragon. Inspired by the building's architecture, they have hit upon the novel idea of having The Godalming Community Gospel Choir sing from the mezzanine floor above as the clientele sip on Elderbubble cocktails below. According to one happy customer, 'it's a riot!'

In addition to the reassuringly expensive dining venues, there are plenty of multicultural takeaways to keep the Hoi Polloi content. The warm and welcoming Michelle at the Chinese has the curious combination of a strong Asian accent and equally strong cockney accent making every visit a fascinating experience. She is a Peking duck out of water in Godalming, so to speak. Recently, and against many residents' wishes, the town has acquired a Domino's Pizza and a Gregg's bakery, prompting some to start looking elsewhere to live, such was their disdain.

But Godalming's character after hours cannot be defined by its restaurants. A much fairer reflection can be found in its umpteen pubs and from the characters that often reside there. The Star boasts being a beer house for the last hundred and seventy five years and hosts beer festivals on all the major bank holidays, attracting ale and cider connoisseurs from all over the county. At the last count, it had won the coveted CAMRA pub of the county on no less than three separate occasions, propelling its popularity further. It proves so alluring that people go to extraordinary lengths to be part of it. One such person was so intent on bypassing the busy bar to get to the sun-trapped garden at the back he vaulted the perimeter fence only to land awkwardly and spend the next two months in hospital with a fractured spine.

With its beams playing host to hundreds of breweries' pump clips and its olde worlde feel, it's always a popular destination for both 'mingers' and town visitors alike. Food orders cease at lunchtime, turning the pub into an old fashioned, traditional watering hole which lends to its rustic appeal. But The Star serves a bigger purpose than just getting its locals inebriated, it's also an important venue for Godalming evening activities. Monday nights at The Star are famed for the 'Fiddly Diddlies', a motley crew headed by the multi-talented Kevin that jam with traditional folk instruments. Come hell or high water, they'll be there, plucking and strumming away with varying degrees of success and applause. They're Monday night limpits and regardless whether you love or loathe them, there is no escaping them and as they've been coming for aeons, they're very much the fabric of the pub.

The 'Fiddly Diddlies' aren't the only community group to call The Star home. 'Stitch 'n' Bitch' have also become a familiar sight. Camped in a corner, they nurse their half shandies throughout the evening eyeing anyone who dares eye them. They look as though they've come straight from a 'Prisoner cell Block H' scene. As the name suggests, it's a local group of women that are doing their best to promote the town's dying art of knitting and woe betide anyone who questions their need to take up swathes of space; by all accounts they're skilled with a knitting needle in other ways than just knitting with them. Both groups have decided to practice on Monday evenings which has led to a strange territorial turf war, with each group suspiciously aware of the other. As one 'minger' put it, 'You know you're in Godalming when the two rival gangs are middle-aged knitters and folk musicians.

Unfortunately, some have taken this communal welcoming too far. On countless occasions, the crowded bar has been taken up with ornate, bomb-proof baby carriers, complete with screaming occupant as the 'responsible' parents sit near-by, drinks in hand expecting the over-worked bar staff to fill in as part-time nannies. If the child-catcher lived in Godalming, he wouldn't require his net and would be a very rich alcoholic.

Hot on the Star's heels for evening entertainment is the Red Lion pub, situated just around the corner. Historically, it was the Godalming Grammar School, where another plaque informs that the town's hero, Jack Phillips had been educated there. It's a big building and notoriously difficult to fill meaning the pub changes hands frequently with each new landlord having grand ideas on how to optimise the space. Currently, in a bid to entice punters, it offers an abundance of evening activities from live music to billiards tournaments. There's even live, nude drawing taking place which, sadly, isn't that well attended, although I suspect if they got an attractive woman to pose rather than the usual pot-bellied ageing man they might attract a bigger crowd. But hats off to the present landlords, they couldn't try harder to reinvent and resurrect the fortunes of this historic venue.

Tucked away near the train station lies the Rose and Crown. Again, it's a cosy little pub with its fair share of regulars. Several large screen TVs can be found throughout making it a popular destination when there's a sporting event on, especially football and especially when Manchester United are playing. When punters aren't shaking their fists and swearing at the ref on TV, they're cheering and jeering the darts players in the back room. In such a competitive, alpha-male environment, it's no surprise few women drink there and probably shouldn't be regarded in the running for places to take a first date.

Then there's The Lounge. More of a bar than a pub, it's the only establishment to have bouncers on the door and this is entirely justified as the vast majority of their customers have either been thrown out of other ale houses for misbehaving or are determined to have one last attempt at taking a lucky somebody home for the night. Widely considered to be Godalming's 'meat market', the bar plies patrons with booze until 1 a.m as groups of expectant boys stand near the dance floor, in benign conversation with mates hoping to catch a lady's eye. Predictably, some situations spill over and as a result, the bouncers earn their wage.

Not surprisingly, Friday and Saturday nights are the busiest, a fact not lost on the GOLO agents who circulate the town's pubs selling Godalming lottery tickets. Running since 2008, it is believed to be the first town lottery of its kind and in true Godalming style now accepts payments for its monthly draw through standing orders. The well-intentioned agents are given a somewhat Marmite reception from the regulars but continue about their work with an unflappably cheerful disposition.

Like many mid-sized, friendly towns, life in Godalming is lived in a bubble. Faces around town and particularly in pubs quickly become familiar with personal business inevitably becoming the town's business. Professionally of course, this can be very useful but personally, it can have severe drawbacks. One such example was witnessed by a work colleague returning home after shopping at Waitrose. Part of her evening route took her through the church's unlit graveyard that runs adjacent to a beautiful old building that now hires out office space. On an otherwise very black night, the lights of the top office attracted her attention. As she stood gazing up, she realised she was watching what she guessed to be a young secretary working overtime on her older, female boss. She also then realised that she recognised both of them and had even stopped to chat to them that lunchtime.

Instead of going on her way, she decided to make herself comfortable on a nearby tombstone, crack open a bottle of wine and a packet of digestives and watched to see how things progressed. By the time the lights were switched off, their audience had grown to about six or seven all dotted around the graveyard having Waitrose picnics on the tombstones, and, judging by the excited chatter, the two women seemed fairly well known for reasons other than their late evening performance. It must have come as a surprise to them to see their popularity around town soar in the days that followed and also why the graveyard had become so busy in the evenings.

Healthy, Wealthy and Wise

Despite what the statistics may suggest, it's not cucumber sandwiches, garden parties and lawn bowls for everyone. Godalming, again like most towns, has an eclectic mix of people. For all the millionaires, there are those who are less fortunate and for those poor souls the powers that be are less welcoming, treating them almost as a stain on Godalming's good name.

One current resident gave me an example of this attitude. Having fallen on hard times, he was directed by the town's Citizens' Advice Bureau to enquire at the Council offices to see what might be available to him. He duly took their advice and attended a meeting with one of the housing officers. After he told the officer of the luck that had befallen him, he was offered a one-way bus ticket to a hostel in Slough. Yes, Slough of all places. When he asked what was to happen to him thereafter, he was told in no uncertain terms that he would be Slough's responsibility. Having friends and family in Godalming he turned the generous offer down and at that the housing officer abruptly closed his file and left the room, leaving him to contemplate which bridge would be most suitable to sleep under in the meantime.

Thankfully, he weathered that particular storm but it left a big question mark over those residents that don't have a bursting bank balance and don't have a friends and family support network. Is it simply a case of if you can't afford to live in the area the authorities will gladly help you pack?

With the Council's dubious duty of care policy, what services are available to the luckless minority? Well, my exploration led me to a workshop offering advice on how to manage life. On arrival, I was shown into a room and waited, not really sure what to expect. As others started to dribble in and take their seats, I became even more intrigued. The first chap that came in gazed around the room as if he had never been in one before. The next person who took a seat next to me was a lady in her forties, although it was difficult to accurately gauge an age as she spent the entire time hiding behind a tissue into which she cried incessantly, not lifting her head once. Then came a relic from the 80's nightclub scene; tie-dyed t-shirt, highlighted perm, baggy trousers and unable to keep still, the woman bounced on and off her chair reaching for the stars as she danced away to an imaginary tune. The last member of the group was clearly foreign and lost but tentatively took her place next to 'disco Sue' and smiled politely when asked if she liked the silent music. What was evident was the fact that even in jeans and a shirt I was very much over-dressed. We waited, each in our own world, for our tutor to appear. Soon after the door opened and in walked a big, black woman, wearing a loud floral dress, high heels and a jaunty red netted fascinator, complete with a miniature top hat, not too dissimilar to that of the Mad March Hare from Alice's Adventures in Wonderland; finished off with bright red lipstick. She beamed in a warm, loving way and welcomed us to her workshop. The other chap in the group stared at her gormlessly, spittle hanging from his gaping mouth. The crying woman sobbed louder, burying her head further into her sodden tissue. 'Disco Sue' then attempted a terrible rendition of Bob Marley's song Redemption whilst the non-English speaking woman looked on, trying to work out what the hell was going on.

(The workshop begins)

Tutor: "Well hello my lovelies.' *(in a strong Caribbean accent)* 'How are we today?"

(Silence from the group)

Tutor: "My name is Marion and you're in a safe place."

(She pauses, taking time to smile at us individually)

Marion: "Now then, what is emotion? Can anyone tell me what an emotion is?"

(She smiles again, pen hovering over the whiteboard. The group remain silent)

Marion: "OK. Let's start from the beginning. E anyone?"

(The woman next to me, sobs louder, burying her head further into her tissue)

Disco Sue: "Yes please."

(She bursts into laughter, waving her hands above her head. Ten minutes in and we finally have the word emotion written on the white board at the front)

Marion: "Can anyone give me an example of an emotion?"

(The man raises his arm)

Marion: "Yes my love."

Man: "Chocolate?"

Marion: "Not quite my love but a very good effort."

(He looks chuffed, shuffling around in his chair)

Marion: "Anyone else?"

Disco Sue: "Dance?" *(again reaching for the stars)*

Marion: "Close my love, we'll
put joy down for that"
*(She scribbles joy on the white
board under emotion)*

Eager to find out where this was going, I kept
quiet.

Marion: "OK my lovelies, we'll leave that
there for now. So, has anyone here heard
the word, meditation? Med...it...a...tion?"
(Blank looks)

Marion: "Meditation can help with difficult
emotions. When we get angry, anger is
an emotion" *(she writes anger underneath
joy)*, "meditation can help calm us down.
I want to take you on a meditation my
lovelies. Come with me to a happy place.
I want you to inhale" *(she slowly but loudly
inhales and then exhales)* "and let it all out.
Good good. Close your eyes and breath,
in" *(inhales loudly)* and out *(exhales loudly)*
"Good good, feel the air rush in. Are you
all comfortable? That's it, in.....out.....in....
out....Now, I want you to imagine yourself
in a beautiful place, a safe place, a golden,
happy place, a place full of piss..."

My eyes open and I'm straight back in the room, questioning whether I had heard her correctly.

> **Marion**: "Good good, that's it,
> feel the piss flow over you, warm,
> golden piss....and exhale."

Her accent had unfortunately given the meditation a whole new meaning.

> **Marion**: "Let the piss flow over you, warm
> piss, golden piss, can you feel my piss, I have
> so much piss to give you. Are you feeling
> my piss, I can feel your piss, mmmm.....
> good, I can feel your piss, all over me.."

I looked around at my fellow peers to see whether I was the only one who was hearing it. The other chap was staring at her, saliva flowing freely from his open mouth, the crying woman had found another gear to her sobbing, disco Sue was laughing and clapping her hands like a deranged toddler repeatedly shouting 'piss piss piss' and the foreign woman was trying to join in with the clapping but was still clearly confused as to what was going on. I hung my head in bemused disbelief.

Finally, the meditation came to an end with the group being far more agitated than it had been at the beginning of the session. The misunderstanding was lost on Marion. She congratulated and thanked everyone for their 'piss' contribution and hoped that when emotions got the better of us, we would close our eyes and think of a safe place full of 'piss'.

On thanking Marion, I was held tightly to her bosom and as I said my goodbyes, she stroked my bald head affectionately. Declining a dance off with disco Sue I left, questioning meditation techniques as well as the services that were provided for the not so blessed folk of the Borough.

This was a one off public service and should be regarded as such. Privately, Godalming has fully embraced alternative health services. Practitioners of all varieties are readily available, charging prices that truly befit the town's wealth. Whilst health prices are, well, healthy, value for money is questionable.

Physically, 'mingers' are in pretty good shape. Of course there are still those that park on the high street, blue badge proudly displayed on their windscreen, that quite literally have to roll themselves out of an impossibly small car, a bit like a space-hopper trying to exit Noddy's car. It's no St Tropez beach party but on the whole people look relatively healthy and with a life expectancy of 81, it seems like a comfortable place to see out your latter years.

Keeping the town fit and healthy is one of the local gyms which has passed through so many hands recently, not even the staff that work there actually know who they're working for. As a result, no one seems willing to invest in it so the place has fallen into slight disrepair.

One cravat wearing, cigar chugging Star regular, Lucian, was keen to share his first-hand gym experience. Large whiskey in hand, plum in mouth, he told his tale.

Lucian: "Well, it occurred after Christmas. I had just spent a very relaxing two weeks in The Omnia...in Zermatt....Switzerland? You must know it? Oh I've been going for years, it's fabulous, you really must go. Anyway the one drawback of The Omnia is the size of the portions, they're huge; absolutely enormous. I can't tell you how many fondues I failed to finish. And then of course there's the cheese boards, the ports, the wine, oh, you know how it is, they almost force feed you the champagne. Bugger the skiing, I only skied once in the entire two weeks that I was there and that's only because Bertie, Bradders and Chappers insisted we all did a heli-drop onto a glacier, off piste.' (smiling and shaking his head wistfully.)'Well, I returned from Zermatt, let's just say, a little more portly than when I had left (rubbing his bulging beer belly) and so thought maybe I should shed a few pounds. If I'm going to give myself a fighting chance of snaring a filly this year I'm going to have to lose a bit of this drag...' (wobbling his stomach up and down, looking at me) 'Oh no, it's not bad, it could just be better. Anyway, off I went, I couldn't be arsed to look around so I just went along to the nearest one and signed up for a free trial, they're all much of a muchness these days. The young man who signed me up had the audacity to ask whether I was familiar with the machines and if I needed an induction! Can you believe that? Cheeky bastard, he's lucky I didn't punch him another arsehole. Anyway, I got changed and made my way over to the cross-trainer for a warm up before I hit the tread-mill and the free weights. I was on to record a personal best, I mean I was flying, when my right hand slips off the handle and whacks me on my forehead, bang in the middle. Well, that catapulted me off the back and onto a tread-mill, somewhat surprising the rather charming young lady who was using it at the time. I was furious, whoever was on it before me clearly hadn't wiped it down. I had a right mind to complain. Humiliated, I went back to the changing room to have a sun bed, for health reasons of course. I'm used to those lie down ones, you know, the normal ones, but this one was a stand up one. I hadn't used one of those before so I dropped my towel, locked the doors behind me and stood there waiting for it to begin. 5 minutes went by, nothing. 10 minutes went by, nothing. The light didn't even come on. When I tried to open the doors, the darn lock thing came off in my hand. I was locked in there, naked, in the pitch black, for the best part of forty five minutes I reckon before the cleaner came to my rescue. When he opened the doors, I naturally gave him a huge hug, as anyone would and do you know what he said to me? Unbelievable. 'Sir, it's customary to take a towel in with you and if you try that on again, I'll report you.' Can you believe that? He'll report me. Me? That's not the end of it.' (getting seriously agitated.) 'I then decided to have a sauna, what could go possibly wrong in a sauna I thought. Well, I wasn't in there long before I was joined by an old duffer. As a general rule, I don't like to make conversation or even eye contact in saunas, I've never really known where to look you see. But this chap, he didn't stop. He was asking questions about the weather, about politics and then out of nowhere, about my love life! Who does that I ask you? When I looked up, he did that awful Sharon Stone leg over thing. You know, when she's in that office? His was far less graceful, let me tell you. His towel, or more like his ill-fitting flannel, shifted during his manoeuvre, landing his flaccid todger on the hot bench. Poor chap, I've never seen someone move so fast. He shot up, smashing his head into the ceiling before doubling over, one hand on head and the other cradling his seared scrotum. While he was tending to his injuries I was behind him, bobbing and weaving trying my best to avoid contact with his wrinkly, sweaty bottom. I'll tell you what though, for an eighty year old he was extraordinarily supple. It made pretty grim viewing. Eventually, he seemed to tire and with rivers of sweat pouring off him he settled back in the corner. I should have just left him there but with his chest heaving, limbs lifeless and scrotum red raw, I felt guilty leaving him and in actual fact became quite worried when he closed his eyes and stopped speaking. After a very brief one-way conversation I thought he might, indeed, actually be dying. I kept repeatedly hitting the emergency button, but again nothing. What's the point of an emergency button if it doesn't work? Eh? Tell me, what... is... the... point? With nobody coming it was left up to me to try and get him out. No matter how hard I tried, I just couldn't get any purchase on him, we must have looked like two eels wrestling. Well, in all the commotion my towel came loose just as the same cleaner reappears to witness me struggling naked with a semi-conscious old man. He had no interest in listening to my side and ran out saying he was going to report me to the manager. What are the chances? I couldn't just leave him in there so I repositioned my towel, propped open the saunas glass door with a stray, misplaced flip-flop to get some air in, and went to find help and explain myself. The only person I found was the same young fellow who had signed me up and after explaining the towel incident, took him back to the changing room to discover another lifeless body, this one bleeding from a cut above his eye, lying outside the sauna. The useless chap didn't know what to do so he headed off to find more help, abandoning me with both bodies. I don't know what he expected me to do. By God's grace it wasn't long before the newest of the bodies began to stir and after reminding him where he was, I politely suggested he replaced his towel and restored some dignity. When I tried to help, in came the cleaner with the manager and the young chap. 'You see, you see' shouted the cleaner, pointing at me helping the poor disorientated fellow, 'he's got another one'. I couldn't believe it. As much as I tried telling them I was helping, they weren't having any of it and made me out to be some sort of sexual pervert. I was the one who should have been getting the apologies. Outrageous. It turns out that the second chap had walked into the sauna door, cut his eye, slipped over and knocked himself unconscious. Well, when questions were raised about how the flip flop came to be wedged under the door I thought it was probably time to leave, so I quietly left them nursing the two recovering casualties whilst I got changed and made a swift exit. I just didn't think it was worth explaining myself. Bastards. On the way out, I was passed by two paramedics, one carrying a stretcher and the other, a large oxygen tank. I'm never going back there again, took months off me that did. The fillies will have to wait. Right, so who wants a drink?"

He left without taking any orders and returned to the bar to refresh his glass.

Whether Lucian's account is to be taken seriously or not, it gives an interesting insight into the local gym and the locals who use it. Unless you're prepared for truly bizarre, even surreal situations, it's probably best to give 'mingers' and their health a wide berth.

Strawberries and Silverware

During the summer months, Godalming hosts Staycation, a free music and arts festival for local people. It attracts all generations and is always well attended. With all day drinking, live music and usually sunny skies, it's a good occasion to people watch and observe Godalming life. The festival takes place down by the river in the Phillips' Memorial Park where acts perform in the centrally positioned bandstand. All attending are encouraged to bring picnics, chairs and anything else they might need for their day's revelling.

Incidentally, back in the summer of 1818, locals were invited to do the same, although not to enjoy the quirky bands playing but to witness the public hanging of two local murderers and it was a sell-out. People came from as far afield as Woking and Hindhead to watch the execution over the river on the Llamas lands, and according to historians, like the present day, had a jolly, fun, festival atmosphere. Folklore has it, that at an angle, the kink in the nearby church spire is a direct result of townspeople removing one of its oak timbers to use as gallows and over time has bowed and warped under the weight of countless, convicted bodies. Architecturally, that's questionable but it's something to dwell upon the next time you notice it.

Thankfully those days are long gone and now the families that gather for Staycation do so for the music. There are all manner of marvellous chairs, head-wear, picnic hampers and sozzled people on show. Again, you know you're in Godalming when you come across bespoke, handmade, wooden La-z-boys, a full six chair dining table(complete with swan napkins and candlestick), a Harrods hamper and my favourite, a sunburnt, half naked, rotund, middle-aged man wearing a rubber chicken hat, face down, passed out in his family's silver punch bowl, straw stuck in his nose. It was quite a sight. Apart from the tennis, it has all the hallmarks of a middle England Wimbledon including the wealthy majority supping exclusively on Champagne, nibbling away on strawberries and laughing unnaturally loudly at things that simply aren't funny. To back this up, I happened to over-hear a conversation between five, well-heeled, ageing ladies, champagne flutes in hand, Ascot hats on heads, six inch heels slowly descending into the turf. It went like this:

Woman one: "How was Queen's this year Meredith?"

*(Meredith lowers her flute and sunglasses
to look at the woman pinching her lips)*

Meredith: "Is that a joke Felicity?"

(Felicity looks stunned)

Felicity: "No, why, what
happened Meredith?"

Meredith: "No one's told you? Well,
you know we have hospitality suites
at both Queens and Wimbledon?"

Felicity: "Yes....and you go every year."

Meredith: "Not this year Felicity."

*(Meredith places her champagne flute on
the table under the cedar framed gazebo.
She seems annoyed, almost angry)*

Meredith: "Strawberries are what
happened Felicity. Strawberries. It was
a bumper crop this year and you know
what Felicity, they won't pick themselves,
will they? I'm surprised no-one told
you about my frightful dilemma."

*(She glowers at the rest of the female
party, who in turn, hang their heads)*

Meredith: "So, to answer your question
Felicity, I don't know how Queens
was, I wasn't there. I'll tell you what,
I'll go and get Godfrey, I'm sure he'll

be able to give you a blow by blow
account on how wonderful it was."

At that, she storms off, presumably in search of Godfrey, leaving Felicity on the verge of tears and in need of comfort from the remaining, shamed group.

In that same afternoon, one well to do woman was watching a talented local choir perform when she brazenly remarked, 'I've never seen so many chavs and chavettes in one place.' She was clearly unaware of any offence she might have caused and was left visibly vexed after receiving a monumental tongue-lashing from one of the choir members' mothers.

Like any festival, the combination of music, sun and alcohol results in reckless behaviour. Staycation and its patrons are no exception. Last year's was particularly eventful. The tone was set relatively early, in fact just after families had packed up all their picnicking paraphernalia, when a young man started dancing naked in the bandstand where two hours earlier, tots were wobbling away to a Peppa Pig song. His solo performance had not gone unnoticed by the two attending policeman who approached him with such caution you would think he was a human hand-grenade. After a couple of minutes of fruitless negotiation and more dancing, one of the officers flung himself at the gyrating whippersnapper and successfully pulled him to the floor so that his companion could cuff him. Once cuffed he was led away, still naked out one of the park's shady side entrances so as not to offend any residents that might happen to be overlooking the park.

The next drunken misdemeanour occurred shortly after the officers had left with their stumbling quarry. Majestic weeping willows hug the riverside that runs adjacent to the park; their long, overhanging branches offering protection to the walkers and riverbank fauna below. On any given day in the year, its calming serenity makes it a memorable journey for all ages. Any day but this one. The peace had been interrupted by three well lubricated teenagers on a home-made raft attempting to row upstream. Clearly the raft had been hastily built as it consisted of a Waitrose shopping trolley, one rusty barrel and the remains of a wooden chair, all lashed together with green riverbank reeds. Their progress wasn't so much slow as non-existent and regardless of how hard they rowed, their squash racquet oars did little to progress them or indeed stop them sinking. The best indication to how drunk they were was only fully realised after the river swallowed their raft. Too fuddled to notice they were no longer afloat, they carried on their determined rowing with no less vigour. By now they were essentially swimming with squash racquets and only conceded defeat after one of the resident swans took exception to them sharing its water.

The final folly that day belonged to a middle-aged man wearing a tie around his head. From the outset it didn't look good. Hopping on one foot he seemed intent on executing a move that can only be described as the human hoola hoop. In theory, it's straightforward. By holding your right foot with your left hand you create a hole which you try to get the rest of the body through. In practice, it's an impossibility of course but after copious amounts of booze in the mid-summer sun, the enthusiastic gent seemed to think it was more than possible and kept throwing himself into a heap one failed attempt after the other. The small but vocal crowd that had gathered were doing nothing to dampen his spirits, in fact, quite the contrary. In unison they were giving him a countdown from three and as he once again clambered back to his feet, eagerly pointing out that he needed more height in his leap. He took their words as gospel and did indeed continue to jump higher only to land more heavily each time. Well, eventually lady luck ran out of patience with him and after a particularly large leap, landed or should I say crumpled, on his ankle, quickly dispersing the muted crowd. With his right foot now at a very unnatural angle, his human hoola hooping was over for the day. As one concerned, departing woman called the ambulance, he was left sitting on the grass, staring at his foot, trying to work out why his toes were pointing behind him.

Whilst alcohol is a great leveller, you know when you're in Godalming when poverty is not measured by how many cans of Special Brew residents can afford but by how many bottles of wine are in the wine rack. Let me give you an example. I was invited around to a resident's house for a cup of tea. It was a beautiful semi-detached, three storey town house, with an extensive back garden that snaked up a hill to a decked platform and a modest summerhouse allowing sensational views over the town and the surrounding area. In 2014, the average price for a property like this in Godalming was in the region of £450,000, although with its location and vistas, this house would have been considerably more. We took in the views as we sipped our tea, marvelling at the scenery. It was then that my host, informed me that she was living in poverty. She was a divorcee, didn't work and was looking forward to her third and final child reaching adulthood and flying the nest which would ease her financial strife. As the sun set, we made our way back down the garden, collecting firewood to burn on the open fire. Concerned by her latest revelation, I sensitively asked her about the mortgage situation,

Her: "Oh no darling. No mortgage, no debt, never done debt. I do have my father's inheritance to come, so I suppose that will keep the wolf from the door."

Me: "I'm not sure whether that constitutes poverty does it?"

(She looked at me as if I had just given her an STD)

Her: "Look!" she said sternly, eyes narrowing, pointing to a nearly full, bespoke mahogany wine rack. "How many Pinot Noirs do you see in there Ben? How many?"

Me: "Um, not sure, none?"

(She shakes her head, clearly offended)

: "No Ben two, only two. There should be at least half a dozen in there. I never thought I would ever get to this"

(She sighs heavily, head in her hands)

Me: "I don't understand", sure that I was missing something.

Her: "Ben, that should be full. Look at it,
go on, have a good look, you see, only
two. It's not funny, this is serious."

Our respective silences were only broken when she
asked me to open a 2006 Rioja reserva, which was
then promptly followed by another. She remarked
that we had to finish the second otherwise it would
be thrown away.

Aside from this perceived poverty, there is a
genuine case for poverty in Godalming. The
Godalming Health Check report noted that 'A
small area of the town is deemed to be the most
deprived in Waverley and the sixth most deprived
in the whole of Surrey' and due to expense of the
limited housing 'There is an insufficient supply
of lower priced accommodation in the owner
occupied sector and a shortage of affordable
housing either for rent or shared-ownership in
the housing sector'. There is a growing, collective
concern that young professionals are being priced
out of Godalming, leaving the town with a retired,
ageing population. This has not gone unnoticed by
Waverley Borough Council, but surprisingly and
worryingly 'a substantial proportion of the housing
stock owned by Waverley Borough Council fails
to meet the Decent Homes Standard and that the

Authority continues to struggle to find the funds to bring the housing stock up to standard.'

In a wealthy town like Godalming, with million pound mansion owners pleading poverty, I wonder whether sub-standard housing is defined as 'without a wine cellar'?

Great Expectations

Without question, 'mingers' are proud of their town and its splendid past. Testament to this is Godalming museum, which is run by passionate volunteers who continually research and update their records with all things Godalming. Nondescript and with an unassuming entrance it opens up to be a tardis of a building on two floors that enjoys a well-kept secluded garden where visitors can sit for tea and cakes.

Throughout the year, they run different exhibitions, celebrating Godalming's involvement in formative events in history. Its many hidden away drawers and cupboards contain everything from Jekyll blueprints to obscure court records.

On the upper landing, there is even a Godalming Hall of Fame which is divided into vocations, with poor old Mary Toft heading up the category 'On the wrong side of the law'. If you do have time to pass, have a look, there are some fascinating and surprising stories of some very unlikely individuals. Hopefully, modern characters such as mad Maureen will make it up onto that glorious Hall of Fame one day; time will surely qualify her as one of Godalming's Greatest. It was here in one of the archives that Charles Softley was stumbled upon. He lived a hundred and fifty years ago and also wrote an account of the town. Measuring only 3'9" in height, he was by today's definition a dwarf and had to sit on a billiards table in order to take a shot. Looking at his photo, he would have been a shoe-in for a hobbit if he was alive today but that doesn't detract from the plentiful information he provided on the town of yesteryear. Let's hope its not another 150 years before somebody else puts pen to paper to describe life in England's greatest, little known town.

According to a recent poll, 97.4% of Godalming's inhabitants are happy with the way things are and are resistant to any change, so it looks like Godalming has more coffee shops, baby shops and charity shops to look forward to, not to mention soaring property prices. One displeased elderly resident, like many others, had made his money in London before retiring to the town for a slower, quieter way of life but has recently become increasingly concerned with the rising property market. His new neighbours just happen to be Russian, putting the fear of God into him that the town is on the frontline of a new cold war. Enquiring about their involvement in local affairs, his answer was somewhat baffling.

"Absolutely dear boy. Thrice they have been seen at the cheese counter at Waitrose."

That was it. That was his answer. What was clear was the fact that Godalming has now attracted the attention of the super rich and as prices continue to soar, 'mingers' can expect longer queues at the Waitrose deli counters.

Another noticeable change is the evolving skyline. At the time of writing, buildings seem to be popping up everywhere, reluctantly pulling Godalming kicking and screaming into the twenty first century. One of the biggest, recent worries of the town's expansion has been the planning of a new Tesco on the old Godalming Arms site, a stones throw from the already giant Sainsburys and sizeable Waitrose. Despite numerous protests and petitions, permission to build was still granted, infuriating residents as no plans to improve the archaic, overburdened traffic system have been put in place. On the eve of the build, the site was razed to the ground, affording a temporary, yet inevitable reprieve. This unwillingness to accept change may be forcibly short-lived but it is not without genuine and realistic concern for present 'mingers' and the future fortunes of their beloved town. As one Mr William Brinkley said in

September 2013, 'Living in Godalming has been heaven, moving from here will be hell'.

Like most towns these days, much of the community communicate through social media sites and Godalming has a particularly active following. Updates are regularly posted and passionately discussed. Some of the more inflammatory responses quite rightfully came after a posting that Godalming Town Council is planning to spend £3500 of public money on 'recognition badges for wives and consorts of ex mayors.' While Godalming holds the title of the most sought after place to live in the country, it's a far cry from being perfect. To echo many of the replies, there are needier causes to be addressed before accessorizing people with badges. Mad Maureen's footwear must surely be a higher priority.

On a final note, I refer to David Nobbs' footnote in 'The return of Reginald Perrin – 'It is believed that this book mentions Godalming more than any other book ever written, including 'A Social, Artistic and Economic History of Godalming' by E Phipps-Blythburgh.' Mr Nobbs, you may well poke fun at what Godalming has to offer but I do believe this book now mentions it more than any other and with good reason. Godalming is one of the last bastions of a truly middle England and long may that continue.

13302068R00043

Printed in Great Britain
by Amazon.co.uk, Ltd.,
Marston Gate.